The Bill of Rights

PREVENTING CRUEL *and* UNUSUAL PUNISHMENT

THE EIGHTH AMENDMENT

Hallie Murray

E
Enslow Publishing
101 W. 23rd Street
Suite 240
New York, NY 10011
USA
enslow.com

Published in 2018 by Enslow Publishing, LLC.
101 W. 23rd Street, Suite 240, New York, NY 10011

Library of Congress Cataloging-in-Publication Data

Names: Murray, Hallie, author.
Title: Preventing cruel and unusual punishment : the Eighth Amendment / Hallie Murray.
Description: New York, NY : Enslow Publishing, 2018. | Series: The bill of rights | Includes bibliographical references and index.
Identifiers: LCCN 2017001866 | ISBN 9780766085633 (library bound book) | ISBN 9780766087415 (pbk. book) | ISBN 9780766087422 (6 pack)
Subjects: LCSH: United States. Constitution. 8th Amendment—Juvenile literature. | Capital punishment—United States—Juvenile literature. | Punishment—United States—Juvenile literature.
Classification: LCC KF4558 8th .M87 2017 | DDC 345.73/0772—dc23
LC record available at https://lccn.loc.gov/2017001866

Printed in the United States of America

To Our Readers: We have done our best to make sure all website addresses in this book were active and appropriate when we went to press. However, the author and the publisher have no control over and assume no liability for the material available on those websites or on any websites they may link to. Any comments or suggestions can be sent by email to customerservice@enslow.com.

Portions of this book originally appeared in the book *The Eighth Amendment: Preventing Cruel and Unusual Punishment* by Greg Roza.

Photo Credits: Cover, p. 1 View Apart/Shutterstock.com; cover, interior pages (background) A-R-T/Shutterstock.com; cover, interior pages (quill) Leporska Lyubov/Shutterstock.com; p. 5 bikeriderlondon/Shutterstock.com; pp. 10, 19 Universal Images Group/Getty News; p. 11 Interim Archives/Archive Photos/Getty Images; pp. 13, 25 Bettmann/Getty Images; p. 16 Hulton Archive/Hulton Royals Collection/Getty Images; p. 22 NaughtyNut/Shutterstock.com; p. 27 Everett Collection/Shutterstock.com; p. 31 Marie Hansen/The LIFE Picture Collection/Getty Images; p. 35 Davis/TNS/Newscom; p. 37 Hulton Archive/Getty Images; p. 41 WilleeCole Photography/Shutterstock.com.

Contents

INTRODUCTION

During the Revolutionary War, the Founding Fathers witnessed many of their friends and fellow patriots captured by British authorities, held indefinitely without bail, and fined unreasonable sums of money. Others were tortured and put to death for their beliefs. The people who created America's government wanted to protect American citizens from unreasonable and malicious punishment, which is why so many of the amendments in the Bill of Rights have to do with the rights of the accused in criminal cases. Along with the Fourth, Fifth, and Sixth Amendment, the Eighth Amendment to the Constitution was designed to protect people who are accused of crimes from being poorly treated before their trials and from being wrongfully or excessively punished if found guilty.

The Eighth Amendment reads: "Excessive bail shall not be required, nor excessive fines imposed, nor cruel and unusual punishments inflicted." For more than 200 years, Americans have struggled to interpret the meanings of the phrases "cruel and unusual," "excessive bail," and "excessive fines." Many cases regarding the Eighth Amendment have come to the Supreme Court.

Much of the contemporary discussion about the amendment has to do with the death penalty.

An empty courtroom, with seats for an audience, a bench for the jury, a seat for the judge, and a box for witnesses

In the United States, people who commit particularly terrible crimes can be executed by the state. These crimes may include treason, terrorism, spying, or certain cases of murder. Most executions are carried out through lethal injection, where chemicals are injected into an accused person's bloodstream in order to stop his or her heart. It is supposed to be painless and instantaneous.

In 2015, a case regarding lethal injection came in front of the Supreme Court. A year earlier, a man named Charles

Lockett was executed in Oklahoma using a three-drug lethal injection procedure that ended up going wrong. Lockett woke up after he was supposed to be unconscious, and it took him a long time to die. Oklahoma immediately investigated and made some other drug combinations available that might work better.

Yet the drug combination that had caused so many problems in Lockett's case was still being used. Twenty-one death row inmates in Oklahoma sued the state over the fact that they could get the drug combination that Lockett received, but they were not successful. A federal district court and the Supreme Court both ruled that because the inmates could not prove that there was some other drug available at the time, they had no right to request a different drug combination. It was not considered "cruel and unusual" punishment for them to receive the injection that had caused the issues in Lockett's execution.

This case shows that the phrase "cruel and unusual" can be incredibly difficult to define, even in a seemingly straightforward case like the death penalty. Our understanding of what exactly the Eighth Amendment means has changed significantly over the years, but the amendment itself endured over the years and continues to affect our lives today.

CHAPTER ONE

CORPORAL *and* CAPITAL PUNISHMENT

Many Europeans came to America to find a better life, though that doesn't mean that life in the American colonies was easy. Settlers had to contend with a number of challenges, from American Indians who were upset that Europeans had intruded on their land to limited food leading to starvation to illness and disease. But after a while, as more and more colonists came to America, these woes lessened. Instead, other struggles took their place.

Criminal activity is present everywhere there are humans. In small villages in early America, crimes could be dealt with one at a time by a single leader, but more people meant more crime, and more crime meant more established ways of dealing with crimes through punishment. Those accused of crimes and presumed guilty could be forced to pay large fines, suffer torture, and even be executed by the state. Much like today, people disagreed over the effectiveness of these forms of punishment. Some people believed that harsh punishments helped reduce crimes, while others believed they were cruel and inhumane. Many of the laws regarding fines, bail, and judicial punishments in the American colonies were directly influenced by British traditions.

PUNISHMENT IN 17TH AND 18TH CENTURY BRITAIN

By the time European colonies were established in North America, Britain already had a long history of harsh judicial sentences and excessive punishments. In eighteenth-century Britain, there were more than 200 crimes for which capital punishment could be applied. These crimes included offenses as heinous as murder or rape and as minor as stealing a neighbor's animals or chopping down a tree.

Capital punishment occurs when the state kills someone for their crimes; it is also referred to as the death penalty. The term "*capital* punishment" comes from the Latin word *capitalis*, which means "regarding the head," because originally the term applied specifically to executions by decapitation. Today, however, it applies to any method of execution. Crimes to which the death penalty may apply are known as capital offenses. In Britain, one major capital offense was treason, or betraying one's own country.

The British government also had a long list of offenses that could result in corporal punishment. Corporal punishment is the administration of pain as a punishment for breaking a rule or law. The term "*corporal* punishment" comes from the Latin word *corporalis*, meaning "body." Thus "corporal punishment" means punishment of the body, through pain. Once again, traitors, or those who had committed treason, were among the most heavily penalized, but people who had offenses such as theft and forgery were often forced to submit to corporal punishment as well. In those days, corporal punishment could mean anything from amputating a hand to cutting someone's nose off to branding with a hot iron.

THE CASE OF TITUS OATES

During the late 1600s, the Anglican priest Titus Oates became the focus of a scandal in Britain. Oates was angered by the recent leniency that King Charles II had shown for Catholicism. In 1678, Oates reported a false account of a "Popish plot" planned by Catholics to assassinate Charles II. As a result, at least fifteen people whom Oates accused were put on trial and executed for treason. Soon, however, it became clear that Oates had made up the story, so he was fined £100,000 ($152,814) and put in prison.

In 1685, James II—a Catholic—became King of England. In retaliation, James quickly had Oates retried for a number of crimes he had been arrested for earlier in life, including public drunkenness and theft. Oates was also found guilty of perjury for making false accusations against Catholics. Oates could not be sentenced to death simply for perjury, so the judge presiding

Titus Oates (1649–1705) is shown here being interrogated by the King's Council in 1678. He is the second person from the right. King Charles II can be seen on the left side of the woodcut sitting on his throne.

over his case instead invented a punishment so harsh many believed Oates would not survive it.

Oates' clerical status was stripped from him, he was heavily fined, and he was sentenced to life in prison. In the weeks after he was convicted, Oates was subjected to frequent pillorying and public beatings. It was decreed that he would undergo the same punishment once a year. Though the case of Titus Oates was not unusual at the time, it was later cited as an example of cruel and unusual punishment by the authors of the English Bill of Rights, discussed in the next chapter.

TREATMENT OF CRIMINALS IN EARLY AMERICA

Punishment in the American colonies was hardly more humane than it was in England. Hanging was the most common form of capital punishment in the colonies. Imprisonment was usually reserved for political hostages and criminals who had money to pay fines. Criminals who had no money were often put to death instead of imprisoned, as few colonists wanted to care for criminals who couldn't afford to pay for their own food and lodging.

THE PILLORY.

As this woodcut's caption indicates, this is an example of the pillory, a wooden frame that traps the victim's head and hands. Sometimes people would throw things, like rotting vegetables, at prisoners in the pillory as a further punishment.

THE SALEM WITCH TRIALS

One of the most notorious accounts of cruel and unusual punishment in the British colonies is that of the Salem witch trials of 1692. The puritans who had settled Salem passed down strict laws against "consorting with the Devil," and in 1692 many residents began to believe that some of their neighbors had broken those laws when two young girls began acting very strangely. Their doctor deduced that the cause was supernatural, which resulted in a wave of paranoia in Salem, and residents began accusing people of witchcraft. Between March 1 and September 22, 1692, thirteen women and six men were put on trial for witchcraft. The accused were given no rights, offered no bail, and subjected to humiliating and sometimes painful punishments. In the end, eighteen of the accused were put to death by hanging. In one instance, heavy stones were placed on top of a man in order to torture him into confessing. He died from the pressure before testifying. In addition, many others—perhaps as many as 200 people—were imprisoned without bail for witchcraft, and some died in jail, largely because there were no laws preventing cruel and unusual punishment at the time.

In early American society, common forms of corporal punishment included pillorying, flogging, branding, and ear cropping. Some people who were perceived to have committed a crime were subjected to torture, which was

The women on the left of this painting of a Salem witch trial appear to be possessed. They point into space, as if pointing out a demon or other apparition in the air.

not considered cruel or unusual if it resulted in a confession. Forms of torture included the use of thumbscrews, starvation, and piling weights on the person's chest until he or she confessed. These methods were believed to be highly successful, but many people confessed to crimes they didn't commit simply to end the torture.

A NEW PERSPECTIVE

While judicial punishment in the colonies may sound cruel and unusual to us, the people of that era had a different perspective. Law enforcement in the colonies was not like it is today. People didn't have a police force to keep them safe. Jails and prisons were uncommon. It was much easier to commit a crime and get away with it. Therefore, many law-abiding citizens felt harsh punishments were just if they deterred crime. Yet in the late seventeenth century, many colonists and British citizens began to feel judicial punishment was often excessively barbaric and unfair. There were few standards regarding proper punishment and fines. The few laws there were regarding punishment, bail, and fines were often completely ignored by corrupt leaders. As the voices of the citizens grew louder, the governments started to listen and take action.

CHAPTER TWO

ORIGINS *of the* EIGHTH AMENDMENT

The Revolutionary War began in 1775. Englishmen living in the colonies started to fight against the English government for denying them certain rights. But soon, these English rebels began to think of themselves not as British citizens fighting for their rights, but as Americans fighting for their freedom. In 1783, America became independent from its mother country. The Founding Fathers realized that they needed to create some kind of government for their new nation. After a failed attempt at government called the Articles of Confederation, they came up with our Constitution. Soon after, the Bill of Rights was added.

These documents represented a giant move away from British rule, though the Founding Fathers were

King John (1157–1216) signs the Magna Carta in 1215. This image depicts King John as very unhappy, because he was somewhat forced into signing the document by his nobles.

also heavily influenced by two major British law documents: the Magna Carta of 1215 and the Bill of Rights of 1689. In England, these documents set limitations on the powers of the monarchy and increased the powers of Parliament, which represented the rights of the people. Since the American government would be a government by the people and for the people, such documents provided much of the inspiration for America's early laws.

THE MAGNA CARTA (1215)

In 1215, British nobles were upset with King John. They accused the king of imposing unfair taxes and using his position to place himself above the law. In order to stop King John from doing these things, the nobles drafted a document called the Magna Carta, the "Great Charter." With the backing of the Catholic Church, they forced King John to sign it.

The Magna Carta listed a set of laws based on earlier documents and traditional laws. Most importantly, it established that the king was not above the law. Before this, the king was thought to have been chosen by God, and therefore he did not have to follow the laws that applied to lesser folk. The Magna Carta changed all this, and as such has had a major impact on the world through the years, including on the Constitution. It set the precedent of recording human rights in the form of laws.

The Magna Carta was also one of the earliest inspirations for the Eighth Amendment, because it states that a man accused of a crime should receive punishment equal to his crime in the form of an amercement, or a fine imposed as a punishment. Criminals should not have to suffer through just any punishment. The severity and type of punishment should instead match the crime committed.

THE ENGLISH BILL OF RIGHTS (1689)

In 1688, the Parliament (and angry citizens) forced King James II from the throne for abusing the powers of the monarchy. Parliament then asked James II's daughter Mary and her husband, William of Orange, to take the throne. However, Parliament also insisted that the new monarchs sign a new document called the English Bill of Rights, which made Parliament more powerful than any single monarch. It also stated that the people had specific rights that no king or queen could take away.

The phrase "cruel and unusual punishment" was also first used in the English Bill of Rights, which said "the bill of rights has particularly declared that excessive fines ought not to be imposed, nor cruel and unusual punishments inflicted." The first time the phrase was used in the United States was in the Virginia Declaration of Rights of 1776, written by George Mason. This language would later make its way into the Eighth Amendment to the Constitution.

Shortly after the British Parliament passed the 1689 Bill of Rights, Titus Oates, the Anglican priest mentioned in the previous chapter, petitioned both Houses of Parliament to release him from prison. He argued that his punishment was cruel and unusual and that his fine was excessive. However, the members of one of the Houses of Parliament, the House of Lords, believed him to be insane and better off in prison. Furthermore, they believed his punishment was appropriate based on the fact that his actions led to the deaths of fifteen people.

Benjamin Franklin was a Founding Father, printer, inventor, scientist, and writer. He helped draft the Constitution.

Members of the other House, the House of Commons, decided to release Oates. In speaking with the members of the House of Lords, they agreed that there was no precedent for the punishment in common law. They also believed that Oates's punishment set a bad example for future cases. If his punishment was not condemned as excessive, as well as cruel and unusual, what would stop Parliament from imposing similar punishments on people in the future? Oates was released soon after.

WRITING AND AMENDING THE CONSTITUTION

After the failure of the Articles of Confederation, the Founding Fathers met in Philadelphia to draft a new

AN EARLY HISTORY OF BAIL

The first British bail laws, which originated as far back as the thirteenth century, were frequently abused over the years. Bail and fines were often excessively high, and bail was frequently withheld altogether. In the early seventeenth century, King Charles I expected certain nobles to give him loans. When they did not, he imprisoned them without bail or trial. Even when Parliament sought to create laws protecting the right to reasonable bail—as in the Petition of Right of 1628 and the English Bill of Rights of 1689—the king often found ways around the law. Early U.S. bail laws—including those in documents like the 1641 Massachusetts Body of Liberties—were based on British laws and were often broken in similar fashion. Accused criminals were sometimes held without bail and trial for an indefinite period of time. Even after the Eighth Amendment became law, many people questioned exactly what "excessive bail" meant. Some argued that dangerous criminals did not deserve the right to bail, regardless of what the law said.

The Bill of Rights

document, the Constitution. The Constitution as written by James Madison advocated a strong federal, or central, government. However, some of America's leaders felt that the document gave the federal government too much power. They wanted to change, or amend, the Constitution to ensure that the federal government would not be more powerful than individual state governments.

The men who felt the Constitution should be ratified without the Bill of Rights were called Federalists, and they included Alexander Hamilton, James Madison, and John Jay (the authors of the Federalist Papers). The men in favor of adding a Bill of Rights were called Anti-Federalists, and they included Patrick Henry and Samuel Adams. George Mason even refused to sign the Constitution if it didn't include a declaration of rights. Eventually, Anti-Federalist concerns were addressed by the addition of the Bill of Rights to the U.S. Constitution.

One of the primary Anti-Federalist concerns was the treatment and rights of the accused. This is reflected in the Fourth through Eighth amendments. Many of the Founding Fathers felt it was important to include a law against cruel and unusual punishment. Others, however, thought the amendment was too vague to be truly effective. They argued that "excessive" and "cruel and unusual" could mean different things to different people.

The men who drafted the U.S. Constitution took the language for the Eighth Amendment from the Virginia Declaration of Rights. However, Mason suggested an important change. The Virginia Declaration of Rights stated that "excessive bail ought not be required, nor excessive fines imposed, nor cruel and unusual punishment inflicted." Mason wanted the language of the Eighth Amendment to be more direct. He changed it to: "Excessive bail shall not be required, nor excessive fines imposed, nor cruel and unusual

This statue can be found on the National Mall in Washington, D.C. It depicts George Mason, the famous Virginian statesman and staunch Anti-Federalist.

punishment inflicted." By changing "ought not" to "shall not," Mason hoped to create a stronger, more effective law, though the meanings of "cruel," "unusual," and "excessive" remain difficult to determine.

THE JUDICIARY ACT OF 1789

Some critics of the new Constitution argued that while the Eighth Amendment clearly protected citizens from excessive bail, it did not necessarily protect them from the refusal of bail. It quickly became clear that the Eighth Amendment required further legislation to help define the meaning of "excessive." Did it apply to the amount of bail, or was it a question of whether a defendant had the right to bail at all?

On September 24, 1789—just three days after the Bill of Rights was ratified—the U.S. Congress passed the Judiciary Act of 1789. This act established the structure of the U.S. court system, including the Supreme Court and smaller judicial districts. It also outlined the crimes for which bail could be offered and set limits on bail amounts. The act stated that bail would be available to those accused of any noncapital crime. For capital offenses, the decision to grant bail would be left up to the judge presiding over the case. Although the Supreme Court would be called upon again and again to reassess the meaning of the Eighth Amendment, as well as the Judiciary Act of 1789, federal bail law would remain largely untouched for the next 177 years.

CHAPTER THREE

NEW DEFINITIONS *from the* SUPREME COURT

Although the Eighth Amendment was meant to limit the bloody punishments favored by people in the 1700s, painful punishments like pillorying, whipping, and branding, remained regularly in practice for decades after the Constitution was written. The punishment for stealing something, for example, sometimes included 39 lashes with a whip. Although today these punishments would certainly be considered cruel and unusual, they were considered acceptable, even necessary, just 200 years ago.

The rights guaranteed by the Bill of Rights, including the Eighth Amendment, also did not apply to every person in the United States. The Constitution did not recognize slaves, indentured servants, women, or people who didn't own land as citizens. Slavery remained legal in the United States for 75 years after the U.S.

Constitution was ratified. People believed slaves were less than human, and therefore did not deserve basic human rights. They were routinely subjected to beatings, torture, and execution. The growing abolition movement sought to drj9

aw attention to the cruel and unusual punishment that many slaves had to endure, but slavery was an industry that remained entrenched in the American economy for years to come.

HORSE-MARKET

SLAVES HORSES & OTHER CATTLE TO BE SOLD AT 12 OC.

THE LIBERATOR.

VOL. I.] WILLIAM LLOYD GARRISON AND ISAAC KNAPP, PUBLISHERS. [NO. 17.

BOSTON, MASSACHUSETTS.] OUR COUNTRY IS THE WORLD—OUR COUNTRYMEN ARE MANKIND. [SATURDAY, APRIL 23, 1831.

THE LIBERATOR IS PUBLISHED WEEKLY AT NO. 11, MERCHANTS' HALL.

WM. LLOYD GARRISON, EDITOR.

TERMS.

☞ Two Dollars per annum, payable in advance.
☞ Agents allowed every sixth copy.
☞ No subscription will be received for a shorter period than six months.
☞ All letters and communications must be POST PAID.

AGENTS.

CHARLES WHIPPLE, *Newburyport, Mass.*
JAMES E. ELLIS, *Providence, R. I.*
PHILIP A. BELL, *New-York City.*
JOSEPH CASSEY, *Philadelphia, Pa.*
HENRY OGDEN, *Newark, N. J.*
WILLIAM WATKINS, *Baltimore, Md.*

THE LIBERATOR.

'Is not the plea, that emancipation is impracticable, the most impudent hypocrisy and the most glaring absurdity ever propounded for contemplation?—Can any suppositious expediency, any dread of political disorder, or any private advantage, justify the prolongation of corruption, the enormity of which is unequalled, or repel the holy claim to its

two committee men and a constable interfered, and would not permit him to take his seat! He was finally driven away, and the pew passed into other hands.

We purpose shortly to visit all our meeting-houses, and ascertain what places are provided for the accommodation of our colored people. A house dedicated to the worship of Almighty God, should be the last place for the exercise of despotic principles.—But here is the extract:

'With deep regret we have observed some articles in the columns of the "Liberator," of Boston, apparently from this city, in which its inhabitants are implicated; and which we believe the editor of that publication will deem very injudicious, as well as unkind, when knowing the truth in the case. So far from wishing to deprive the colored population of an opportunity to worship God, by the co-operation of the friends of religion with that part of the inhabitants, a good and convenient house was erected a few years since; clergymen of different denominations have often officiated, gratuitously, from Sabbath to Sabbath; and when disappointed in the labors of a Minister, lay brethren have attended at their request, and made exertions to promote the prosperity of their congregation; for many years a Sabbath School has been taught, composed entirely of colored children and adults; in addition to this, if we mistake not, at their request the public

be elevated and improved in this country; unanimous in opposing their instruction; unanimous in exciting the prejudices of the people against them; unanimous in apologising for the crime of slavery; unanimous in conceding the right of the planters to hold their slaves in a limited bondage; unanimous in denying the expediency of emancipation, unless the liberated slaves are sent to Liberia; unanimous in their hollow pretence for colonizing, namely, to evangelize Africa; unanimous in their *true motive* for the measure—a terror lest the blacks should rise to avenge their accumulated wrongs. It is a conspiracy to send the free people of color to Africa under a benevolent pretence, but really that the slaves may be held more securely in bondage.* It is a conspiracy based upon fear, oppression and falsehood, which draws its aliment from the prejudices of the people, which is sustained by duplicity, which is impotent in its design, which really upholds the slave system, which fascinates while it destroys, which endangers the safety and happiness of the country, which no precept of the bible can justify, which is implacable in its spirit, which should be annihilated at a blow.

These are our accusations; and if we do not substantiate them, we are willing to be covered with

virtue. I doubt not this conviction will ultimately prevail in every community, where the obligations of religion and philanthropy are acknowledged; though the process may be slow; having to contend with much ignorance prejudice and error. This conviction, however, is but the first step towards a result so desirable as the total abolition of slavery. Every long established custom acquires a strong hold on the feelings of those who are habituated to its control; we know that its power in many cases is almost unconquerable; and this is especially the case, where a custom, however injurious in its tendencies, is a source of pecuniary emolument, or worldly aggrandizement to those interested in its continuance. It therefore becomes necessary for the attainment of this great and good object—the universal emancipation of our colored brethren—the complete overthrow of this abominable traffic in human flesh—to investigate the whole subject fairly and calmly; to discuss it fully and freely; to ascertain, as far as possible, what are the best means and methods for the accomplishment of this great end. On this point, I find there is great diversity of opinion. Men of equal talents, equal piety, and equal benevolence, take different and almost opposite views of the whole subject: my mind has been much perplexed, by hearing what seemed

***The Liberator* was an abolitionist newspaper published weekly by William Lloyd Garrison and Isaac Knapp from 1831 to 1865. It also championed women's rights long before the cause was popular.**

THE LONG ROAD TO REFORM

Throughout the nineteenth century, the American perspective on what was excessive, cruel, and unusual punishment continued to change. On the legal level, however, these changes moved slowly, as it was sometimes unclear whether such changes were the responsibility of state or federal governments.

In the early 1800s, some groups spoke out against corporal and capital punishment. Most of the developments regarding the death penalty occurred at the state level, and punishments were rarely considered cruel and unusual by state courts. In the early 1800s, most states began passing laws that restricted the use of capital punishment to only the most heinous crimes, particularly rape, murder, and treason. Public whipping was outlawed in 1839. In 1852, Rhode Island became the first state to outlaw the death penalty. Wisconsin followed in 1853. Other states abolished the death penalty as well, but over time, most of them reinstated it.

However, attempts at reform met many obstacles. Much of the nation, including the federal government, was focused on the burgeoning abolition movement, the Civil War, and the period of Reconstruction that followed. For example, President Abraham Lincoln suspended the rights of prisoners during the Civil War, allowing military leaders to arrest civilians and hold them indefinitely without the benefit of a fair trial. Many saw this as unconstitutional, while others felt it was a necessary act in a time of war.

FACING THE FIRING SQUAD

The first significant Supreme Court case regarding cruel and unusual punishment occurred in 1878. The law in the Utah Territory at that time stated that the punishment for a convicted murderer was death by firing squad or hanging.

Execution by firing squad was a method of capital punishment common in wartime or military situations. A number of people would line up and shoot all at once, so no one would know who had actually killed the prisoner.

Wallace Wilkerson, a man convicted of murder and sentenced to death by firing squad, argued that this method of execution constituted cruel and unusual punishment. He appealed the territory's decision to execute him in this way.

The U.S. Supreme Court denied Wilkerson's appeal. It ruled that since the firing squad did not entail a form of torture before death, it could not be considered cruel and unusual. Wilkerson was executed by firing squad on May 16, 1879. Despite the ruling that death by firing squad was not cruel or unusual, reports say Wilkefrson suffered for 27 minutes before he finally died. This case marked an end to the federal government's silence regarding the Eighth Amendment. Furthermore, it validated a decision regarding capital punishment made at the state level. Other important changes would follow in the years to come.

FROM PUBLIC TO PRIVATE EXECUTIONS

By the 1890s, many states had passed laws limiting the number of criminal offenses subject to capital punishment. However, it wasn't until 1897 that the federal government officially limited capital offenses to treason, murder, and rape. It also decided that a jury had the power to rule that the defendant was guilty of a capital offense without imposing a capital punishment; instead, a guilty verdict could result in a life sentence.

Another gradual change was the shift away from public executions, which were often witnessed by large crowds. Executions in the United States had long been a public affair and were intended to serve as a warning for other criminals.

IS EXECUTION "CRUEL AND UNUSUAL"?

In another attempt to make capital punishment more humane, officials in New York State suggested the use of electricity to execute criminals. The first person sentenced to the electric chair was William Kemmler of Buffalo, New York. In 1889, Kemmler killed his common-law wife with a hatchet. After sentencing, Kemmler challenged the ruling, stating that electrocution qualified as cruel and unusual punishment. It is important to note that Kemmler challenged the method of execution but not the death penalty itself. In 1890, the Supreme Court ruled that a method of execution could not be deemed cruel and unusual, or considered a form of torture, as long as it is quick and humane. Specifically, the court decided that electrocution, although untested on humans, was a humane form of execution. The ruling set a precedent regarding the Eighth Amendment. It said that the death penalty itself was not cruel or unusual, but the method of execution could be. Since this ruling, no method of execution has been deemed unconstitutional by the Supreme Court.

The Bill of Rights

By the 1830s, many death penalty opponents were beginning to speak out against public executions, especially hangings, which could result in a slow, agonizing death. Finally in the 1890s, the Supreme Court suggested that public executions should be given up in favor of controlled executions with a limited number of spectators. This decision was made in hopes of "civilizing" capital punishment.

The Supreme Court's decision on the matter of public executions took many years to catch on at the state level across the nation. One of the last public executions was a public hanging that occurred on August 14, 1936, in Owensboro, Kentucky. Eighteen months after it occurred, the Kentucky State Legislature passed a law banning public executions.

EXTENDING THE EIGHTH TO THE STATES IN *FRANCIS V. RESWEBER*

In 1946, 16-year-old Willie Francis was convicted of murder in Louisiana and sentenced to death by electric chair. Due to a malfunction with the equipment, Francis received a shock but did not die. While authorities were planning a second date of execution, Francis's lawyer appealed to the Supreme Court, saying that to attempt to execute Francis a second time would be cruel and unusual punishment and therefore unconstitutional.

In the case of *Francis v. Resweber*, the Supreme Court ruled 5–4 that sending Francis to the electric chair a second time did not violate the Constitution. Francis was successfully executed in May 1947. While the Supreme Court decided not to overturn the conviction, one of the dissenting justices who heard the case, Justice Harold Burton, believed that the Eighth Amendment should apply to the states. This marked the first time the court assumed that the Eighth Amendment extended to state as well as federal governments.

Burton wrote: "It is unthinkable that any state legislature in modern times would enact a statute expressly authorizing capital punishment by repeated applications of an electric current separated by intervals of days or hours until finally death shall result." Although execution by electrocution was considered acceptable under the Eighth Amendment, Burton believed that repeated electrocution was closer to torture and therefore inhumane.

Harold H. Burton was a senator for Ohio from 1941 to 1945 and a Supreme Court Justice from 1945 to 1958 under President Harry Truman.

BAILS AND FINES IN *STACK V. BOYLE*

To this day, there is no uniform set of rules governing bail. Each state has its own set of guidelines. Furthermore, judges can set an excessively high bail, or even deny bail altogether, if they feel the defendant could pose a risk to the community if set free. Some feel this is a violation of the Eighth Amendment.

The first reassessment of the meaning behind the excessive bail clause did not occur until 1951—162 years after the Judiciary Act of 1789 was passed. That year, 12 people were arrested and charged with violating the Smith Act, which made it an offense to belong to an association that advocated the violent overthrow of the U.S. government. At first, each defendant received a different bail amount, ranging from $2,500 to $100,000. Then, bail was set at $50,000 for each defendant. In the case of *Stack v. Boyle*, the defendants attempted to have the bail lowered on the grounds that it was excessive according to the Eighth Amendment. The district court denied the motion, as did a court of appeals.

The Supreme Court found that the bail amount was much higher than previous amounts for similar cases and that the district court did not explain the reason why. They ruled that a bail of $50,000 was excessive, given the limited financial resources of the defendants and the lack of proof that the defendants would flee before their trials. This ruling defined what "excessive bail" means today.

CHAPTER FOUR

The EIGHTH AMENDMENT TODAY

Americans' understanding of what kinds of punishments are "cruel and unusual" or "excessive" has changed dramatically over the years. In the 1958 Supreme Court case *Trop v. Dulles*, Chief Justice Earl Warren emphasized the changing nature of these definitions when he said: "The words of the [Eighth] Amendment are not precise, and their scope is not static. The Amendment must draw its meaning from the evolving standards of decency that mark the progress of a maturing society." That is, it is up to contemporary society to dictate what the meaning of the Eighth Amendment should be. We shouldn't try to guess at what the Founding Fathers might have been thinking, because laws and our attitudes about the best way to respond to criminal activity have changed so much over the years. Of course, there are still disagreements over how to interpret the Eighth Amendment. This is especially true when considering capital punishment, also known as the death penalty.

CAPITAL PUNISHMENT

In 2017, Amnesty International reported that 102 countries had outlawed capital punishment, while another 38 have abolished it in practice. Yet it is still regularly practiced in 58 countries, including the United States. As of 2016, 19 U.S. states and the District of Columbia have outlawed the death penalty, most recently Delaware. Although capital punishment is legal in the other 35 states, many seldom use it, and four (Colorado, Oregon, Pennsylvania, and Washington) had, in 2016, governors who refused to allow prisoners to be executed during their terms. Other states, particularly Texas, are known to make liberal use of the death penalty.

The Supreme Court has made several key rulings on the use of capital punishment. Some rulings reduced or banned the use of capital punishment for youthful offenders, and others banned its use on the mentally disabled. However, two cases in particular were perhaps most influential in shaping the use of the death penalty in contemporary American society: *Furman v. Georgia* and *Gregg v. Georgia*.

Furman v. Georgia

In 1972, the Supreme Court reconsidered capital punishment in three different cases that are together referred to as the *Furman v. Georgia* ruling. The three defendants were not

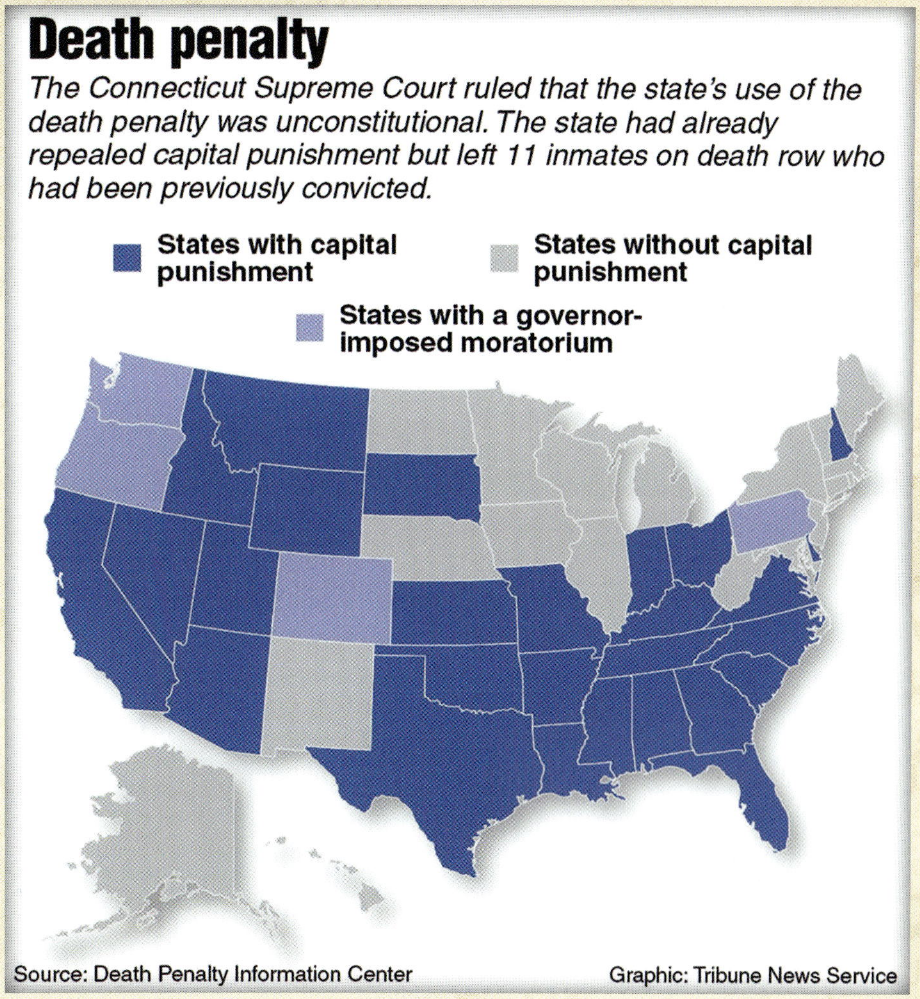

This graphic shows the status of death penalty legislation in various states as of 2015. As you can see, some states have banned capital punishment entirely (gray), some states allow capital punishment but cannot carry out executions due to an order from the governor (in light blue), and others have capital punishment without restriction (dark blue).

connected except by this ruling. They were William Furman, who shot (many say accidentally) the owner of a house he was burglarizing, Lucius Jackson, who was found guilty of rape, and Elmer Branch, who was also found guilty of rape. All three defendants were African American men. This, to many opponents of the death penalty, indicated that capital punishment, like many aspects of the American criminal justice system, had a racial bias to it.

On June 29, 1972, the Supreme Court ruled 5–4 to reverse all three death sentences. They declared that the death penalty was cruel and unusual punishment when applied to these cases. While the ruling itself was rather short, each of the five concurring justices wrote a lengthy statement explaining their personal motives. Several of the justices mentioned racial bias as a contributing factor in their decision. They argued that the use of the death penalty was based solely on the decision of a jury, making it both "capricious" and "arbitrary." Others stated that the death penalty was an outdated method of punishment.

In his statement regarding the *Furman v. Georgia* decision, Justice William J. Brennan Jr.—one of the five concurring judges—declared that there are four principles that help determine if a punishment is cruel and unusual:

- A punishment must not by its severity be degrading to human dignity, especially torture.
- A severe punishment that is obviously inflicted in wholly arbitrary fashion.

- A severe punishment that is clearly and totally rejected throughout society.
- A severe punishment that is patently unnecessary.

In his opinion, these principles prove that the death penalty is unconstitutional.

Justice William Brennan was a Supreme Court Judge from 1956 to 1990. He was a member of the majority that ruled to strike down the death penalty in the *Furman* case.

Gregg v. Georgia

The 1976 Supreme Court case *Gregg v. Georgia* actually involved five separate murder cases. *Gregg v. Georgia* concerned a man named Troy Gregg who was convicted of murder and robbery in a hitchhiking case in Georgia. Under Georgia's revised death penalty laws, a jury first sentenced Gregg to the death penalty, and then an appellate court reviewed the ruling.

By a vote of 7–2, the Supreme Court ruled, in all five cases, that the states had sufficiently changed their laws to ensure that the death penalty could no longer be considered capricious or arbitrary. The seven concurring judges believed that because so many states had revised their death penalty laws, capital punishment was clearly a socially acceptable form of punishment for murders and was therefore not cruel and unusual.

During *Furman v. Georgia*, the Supreme Court ruled that current state death penalty laws were unconstitutional because a jury verdict alone could result in a death sentence. Four short years later, *Gregg v. Georgia* changed all this. The case prompted the states to revise their death penalty laws, which in turn allowed the Supreme Court to redefine the death penalty as constitutional. This outcome has not ended the arguments and controversy surrounding capital punishment, but it has shaped our contemporary understanding of the Eighth Amendment.

THE BAIL REFORM ACTS OF 1966 AND 1984

In 1966, the Supreme Court made the first major change to federal bail law since the Judiciary Act of 1789. The Bail Reform Act of 1966 made the appearance of the defendant at his or her trial the main criteria for granting bail to those charged with noncapital offenses. Courts were instructed to release defendants with the least amount of burden possible to ensure that they actually showed up at their trial. The act did not allow judges to take the chance of danger to people or property into account when setting bail, except for cases involving the death penalty. The Bail Reform Act drew a great deal of criticism. Cases of violent crimes committed by defendants while they were released on their own recognizance increased.

The Bail Reform Act of 1984 changed the 1966 act to allow judges to refuse bail to defendants who posed a threat to the community. Defendants accused of committing

THE EIGHTH AMENDMENT IN ACTION: *ROBINSON V. CALIFORNIA*

In 1962, the Supreme Court made its first ruling officially applying the Eighth Amendment to the states in the case *Robinson v. California*. At the time, California law imposed a mandatory prison sentence for substance addiction. However, the Supreme Court ruled that imprisonment (90 days in this case) for a misdemeanor was cruel and unusual punishment and therefore unconstitutional. The court decided that drug addiction was an illness, and it was unfair to imprison a person simply for being ill, even for a single day. The ruling specified that being addicted to a substance was not the same as selling, buying, or possessing an addictive substance, which were all illegal offenses. The Robinson case also marks the first instance when the Supreme Court ruled that the Fourteenth Amendment covered cruel and unusual punishment. Adopted after the Civil War, the Fourteenth Amendment offers a broad interpretation of U.S. citizenship. Section One of this amendment states that "no State shall make or enforce any law which shall abridge the privileges or immunities of citizens of the United States." According to the Supreme Court's ruling, the actions of the California state government were cruel and unusual and infringed upon the rights and freedoms of a U.S. citizen. The Supreme Court has not yet ruled that the Fourteenth Amendment applies to bail and fines.

The Bill of Rights

violent crimes—crimes requiring a maximum sentence of life imprisonment or death, or drug offenses for which the maximum conviction is greater than ten years, repeat felony offenders, or defendants who pose a risk of flight, obstruction of justice, or witness tampering could be refused bail, because allowing them out into the community might cause more harm. Defendants who do not fit any of these criteria must be offered bail.

In 1986, this act was challenged during the Supreme Court Case *United States v. Salerno*. Anthony Salerno was being held on racketeering charges. He was denied bail because officials believed that he would commit more crimes, including murder, if he was released. Salerno successfully appealed his case to the U.S. Court of Appeals, which declared the 1984 act unconstitutional.

The Supreme Court overturned the decision 6–3. Justice William Rehnquist wrote that the Bail Act of 1984 does not violate the excessive bail clause of the Eighth Amendment. He stated that, "Nothing in the text of the Bail Clause limits permissible government considerations solely to questions of flight." Rather, he added, governments should have the right to deny bail to anyone who poses a risk to the community. The individual right to bail is waived here in order to protect the good of the community

TODAY AND TOMORROW

Today, Americans are as divided about the Eighth Amendment as they were in 1789. Take, for example, the argument

Thanks to the Bail Reform Acts, people cannot be held in jail for more than a given amount of time unless there is a good reason. A "good reason" according to the 1984 Act was if a defendant might cause more harm in the community if they were let out.

for corporal punishment in schools. In 1977, the Supreme Court ruled that it was legal for students in U.S. schools to receive corporal punishments (specifically, paddling). Similar verdicts have been given regarding corporal punishment for criminals in prison. Many think it is perfectly fine, while others find it unconstitutional.

Today, executions are mostly carried out by lethal injection. Many people say that this is more humane than electrocution because it is meant to be painless and fast, but many others say that we have no way of proving that it really is painless and fast. Perhaps one day the death penalty will not exist at all.

Despite differences in Americans' opinions, Supreme Court rulings over the past 50 or 60 years have helped solidify our understanding of what the Eighth Amendment means. This includes not only cases the Supreme Court has overturned, but also cases the Court declined to reverse. As a nation, we have become more humane and fair regarding the rights of the accused. We can thank the framers of the Constitution for having the foresight to protect our most basic rights, even for those who may have broken the law. The Eighth Amendment has served to protect the freedoms enjoyed by American citizens. We will surely hear more on these issues as American beliefs and thoughts on the Eighth Amendment continue to transform in the years to come.

THE BILL OF RIGHTS

First Amendment (proposed 1789; ratified 1791): Freedom of religion, speech, press, assembly, and petition

Second Amendment (proposed 1789; ratified 1791): Right to bear arms

Third Amendment (proposed 1789; ratified 1791): No quartering of soldiers in private houses in times of peace

Fourth Amendment (proposed 1789; ratified 1791): Interdiction of unreasonable search and seizure; requirement of search warrants

Fifth Amendment (proposed 1789; ratified 1791): Indictments; due process; self-incrimination; double jeopardy; eminent domain

Sixth Amendment (proposed 1789; ratified 1791): Right to a fair and speedy public trial; notice of accusations; confronting one's accuser; subpoenas; right to counsel

Seventh Amendment (proposed 1789; ratified 1791): Right to a trial by jury in civil cases

Eighth Amendment (proposed 1789; ratified 1791): No excessive bail and fines; no cruel or unusual punishment

Ninth Amendment (proposed 1789; ratified 1791): Protection of unenumerated rights (rights inferred from other legal rights but that are not themselves coded or enumerated in written constitution and laws)

Tenth Amendment (proposed 1789; ratified 1791): Limits the power of the federal government

Bibliography

Bodenhamer, David J., and James W. Ely Jr., eds. *The Bill of Rights in Modern America*. Bloomington, IN: Indiana University Press, 2008.

Freedman, Russell. *In Defense of Liberty: The Story of America's Bill of Rights*. New York, NY: Holiday House, 2003.

Gaines, Larry K., and Roger LeRoy Miller. *Criminal Justice in Action*. Belmont, CA: Thomson Wadsworth, 2009.

"*Glossip v. Gross*." *Oyez*. Chicago-Kent College of Law at Illinois Tech, n.d. Retrieved December 3 2016 (https://www.oyez.org/cases/2014/14-7955).

Jasper, Margaret C. *The Law of Capital Punishment*. New York, NY: Oxford University Press, 2008.

Little, Rory. "As the 2015 Term opens: The Court's unusual Eighth Amendment focus." SCOTUSblog. September 21, 2015. Retrieved December 2, 2016 (http://www.scotusblog.com/2015/09/as-the-2015-term-opens-the-courts-unusual-eighth-amendment-focus/).

Melusky, Joseph A., and Keith A. Pesto. *Cruel and Unusual Punishment: Rights and Liberties Under the Law*. Santa Barbara, CA: ABC-CLIO, Inc., 2003.

Patrick, John J. *The Bill of Rights: A History in Documents*. New York, NY: Oxford University Press, 2003.

Prinalgin. "George Mason and the Bill of Rights." Associated Content, April 10, 2006. Retrieved January 24, 2010 (http://www.associatedcontent.com/article/26713/george_mason_and_the_bill_of_rights.html?cat=37).

"*Roper v. Simmons*." *Oyez*. Chicago-Kent College of Law at Illinois Tech, n.d. Retrieved December 3, 2016 (https://www.oyez.org/cases/2004/03-633).

"Six Men Legally Killed." *New York Times*. May 17, 1879. Retrieved January 29, 2010 (http://query.nytimes.com/mem/archive-free/pdf?res=9A0CE5DC133EE63BBC4F52DFB3668382669FDE).

Stinneford, John F. "The Original Meaning of 'Unusual': The Eighth Amendment as a Bar to Cruel Innovation." *Northwestern University Law Review*, Vol. 102, No. 4, 2008. University of Florida Levin College of Law Research. Paper No. 2009-26 (http://papers.ssrn.com/sol3/papers.cfm?abstract_id=1015344).

U.S. Supreme Court. "*Furman v. Georgia*, 408 U.S. 238 (1972)." FindLaw. Retrieved February 2, 2010 (http://caselaw.lp.findlaw.com/scripts/getcase.pl?court=US&vol=408&invol=238).

U.S. Supreme Court. "Louisiana ex rel. *Francis v. Resweber* (No. 142) Affirmed. J. Burton, Dissenting Opinion." Cornell University Law School Supreme Court Collection. Retrieved January 31, 2010 (http://www.law.cornell.edu/supct/html/historics/USSC_CR_0329_0459_ZD.html).

U.S. Supreme Court. "*Trop v. Dulles* (No. 70) 239 F.2d 527, reversed." Cornell University Law School Supreme Court Collection. Retrieved January 29, 2010 (http://www.law.cornell.edu/supct/html/historics/USSC_CR_0356_0086_ZO.html).

U.S. Supreme Court. "*Wilkerson v. Utah*, 99 U.S. 130 (1878)." FindLaw. Retrieved January 29, 2010 (http://caselaw.lp.findlaw.com/cgi-bin/getcase.pl?court=US&vol=99&invol=130).

Glossary

abolish To officially end a practice.

appeal A request for, and the hearing of, a previously tried case that can result in a new verdict.

appellate court A court with the power to review and reverse the decisions of lower courts.

arbitrary Randomly chosen.

bail An amount of money that is paid to release a person who has been arrested with the understanding that the accused will appear at a court trial at a future date.

deter To dissuade a person from doing something.

dissent To disagree with.

execution The killing of someone by a state or legislative body.

judicial Relating to a body of judges or the system that administers justice.

legislative Relating to a body of lawmakers or the system of lawmaking.

misdemeanor A crime less serious than a felony that results in less severe punishment.

pillory A wooden frame with holes in which someone's head and hands could be locked.

precedent An action or ruling used to justify future actions and rulings.

racketeering To make money from illegal activities.

ratify To agree to or to make official.

recognizance A formal agreement made before a judge to do something, such as show up for a trial after paying bail.

treason The betrayal of one's country.

Further Reading

BOOKS

Herda, D. J. *The Death Penalty: Furman v. Georgia*. New York, NY: Enslow Publishing, 2017.

Holub, Joan. *What Were the Salem Witch Trials?* New York, NY: Grosset & Dunlap, 2015.

Krull, Kathleen, and Anna DiVito. *A Kids' Guide to America's Bill of Rights.* Revised edition. New York, NY: HarperCollins, 2015.

Quirk, Anne, and Elizabeth Baddeley. *The Good Fight: The Feuds of the Founding Fathers (and How They Shaped the Nation)*. New York, NY: Knopf Books for Young Readers, 2017.

WEBSITES

American Civil Liberties Union (ACLU) Capital Punishment Project

www.aclu.org

The Capital Punishment Project is a national program of the ACLU that conducts public education, advocates reform, and represents defendants convicted of capital crimes.

Death Penalty Information Center (DPIC)

www.deathpenaltyinfo.org

The DPIC is a nonprofit organization that provides the media and public with analysis and information about capital punishment.

National Museum of Crime & Punishment

www.crimemuseum.org

This massive museum includes more than one hundred interactive exhibits and artifacts pertaining to America's history of crime prevention and law enforcement.

Index